The Fourth Floor Twins and the
Disappearing Parrot Trick

———————— In this series ————————

The Fourth Floor Twins and the
Fish Snitch Mystery

The Fourth Floor Twins and the
Fortune Cookie Chase

The Fourth Floor Twins and the
Disappearing Parrot Trick

Also by David A. Adler

The Cam Jansen Adventure Series
Illustrated by Susanna Natti

The
Fourth Floor Twin<u>S</u>

and the
Disappearing Parrot Trick

DAVID A. ADLER
Illustrated by Irene Trivas

Viking Kestrel

VIKING
A Division of Penguin Books USA Inc.
375 Hudson Street, New York, New York 10014
Penguin Books Ltd, 27 Wrights Lane, London W8 5TZ England
Penguin Books Australia Ltd, Ringwood, Victoria, Australia
Penguin Books Canada Ltd, 2801 John Street, Markham, Ontario, Canada L3R 1B4
Penguin Books (N.Z.) Ltd, 182–190 Wairau Road, Auckland 10, New Zealand

Penguin Books Ltd, Registered Offices: Harmondsworth, Middlesex, England

First published in 1986 by Viking Penguin Inc.
Published simultaneously in Canada
Text copyright © David A. Adler, 1986
Illustrations copyright © Irene Trivas, 1986
All rights reserved

Library of Congress Cataloging in Publication Data
Adler, David A. The fourth floor twins and the disappearing parrot trick.
Summary: Two sets of twins launch a wild chase when the "disappearing parrot"
in their school talent show magic act really does disappear.
[1. Twins–fiction. 2. Mystery and detective stories] I. Trivas, Irene, ill.
II. Title. PZ7.A2615FJ 1986 [Fic] 85-40833 ISBN 0-670-80926-8

Printed in the United States of America

Set in Times Roman
3 5 7 9 10 8 6 4

*To Shira Solomon,
Billie and Gabriella*

CHAPTER ONE

"Max, Max!" Donna Shelton called as she ran into the apartment building. "I've been chosen as MC."

Max was painting the frame of one of the lobby windows. He put the brush at the edge of the paint bucket. "MC?" Max asked.

"That's Master of Ceremonies. But for me," Donna said, "I'm a girl—I think it's Mistress of Ceremonies. The fifth grade is having a talent show and I'll introduce all the acts."

The door opened. Donna's twin sister, Diane, walked into the lobby with Gary and Kevin Young.

"Ah," Max said. "My fourth floor twins are all here." Max sat on one of the lobby chairs. He folded his arms and said, "Tell me about this talent show."

Max is the doorman and fix-it man for the apartment building. He calls Donna, Diane, Gary, and Kevin his fourth floor twins because they all live on the fourth floor. And they're twins.

Donna and Diane Shelton are identical twins. But they try not to look exactly alike. Donna wears her hair in braids. Diane's hair hangs straight down. And when they dress in the morning, Diane usually waits to see what Donna is wearing. Then Diane puts on something very different.

Gary and Kevin Young are not identical

2

twins. Gary has curly brown hair and wears eyeglasses. Kevin has straight brown hair and freckles.

"Diane and I are doing a juggling act," Kevin told Max.

Kevin took three plastic bowling pins out of his book bag. He gave one to Diane. He took four giant steps. Then he turned and faced Diane.

"One, two, three," Kevin counted. Then he threw a bowling pin to Diane. She threw

the pin she was holding to Kevin and caught the one flying toward her.

As the bowling pins flew between Kevin and Diane, Gary said, "I'm doing a magic act." He took a deck of playing cards from his pocket and said to Max, "Pick a card and show it to everyone but me."

"Ladies and gentlemen," Donna called out. "Before our next act I'd like to tell you what happened on my way to school this morning."

Max took a card from Gary. He looked at the card, showed it to Donna, and put it back in the deck.

The door opened. "What is this," Mrs. Cooper called out, "a circus tent or the lobby of my apartment building?"

Gary and Donna stopped talking. Diane dropped the bowling pin she was holding. A second pin flew past her and landed near the window, right in the bucket of paint.

Mrs. Cooper was carrying two large shopping bags filled with groceries. Max took one of the shopping bags. The twins watched quietly as Max pushed the elevator button for Mrs. Cooper. The doors opened. Max and Mrs. Cooper walked into the elevator. "The lobby is not a playground," she told the twins as the elevator doors closed.

Diane took the bowling pin out of the bucket. She held it over the newspaper spread near the window. Paint dripped onto the newspaper.

Gary searched through his deck of cards.

"On my way to school," Donna said, "I met a real smart dog. I asked the dog how much four times zero is and the dog said nothing."

"Take a deep breath," someone behind one of the doors in the lobby said.

Gary held up the queen of hearts. "Was this the card?" he asked.

"Yes," Donna told Gary. "That's the card. But did you get my joke? Four times zero is *nothing*. And that's what the dog said. *Nothing*. Get it?"

"There's someone locked behind that door," Kevin said.

"Now listen to this joke about a mixed-up cook," Donna said. "He scrambled his watch and tried to wind up a dozen eggs."

"Quiet," Kevin told the others as he walked toward a closed door. "Listen."

Donna and Gary walked toward the door. Diane didn't. Paint was still dripping from the bowling pin. The twins waited.

"Save me, Doctor. Save me!" they heard someone call from the other side of the door.

CHAPTER TWO

Kevin tried to open the door. It was locked.

"We have to get Max," Donna said. She looked at the lighted number above the elevator doors. "He's on the third floor."

"It's my leg, Doctor. I think it's broken," the twins heard the voice say from inside the closet.

Donna and Gary ran toward the stairs.

"Wait," Kevin said. "The elevator is coming down."

Donna, Gary, and Kevin waited by the elevator door. Diane dropped the bowling pin on the newspaper and waited with them. The door opened and the twins all began talking.

"Max, you have to open that door."

"Someone is locked in there."

"His leg is broken."

"And there's a doctor locked in there, too."

Max smiled and said, "Little Jackie is in there. I put him there so I can look in on him when I'm not busy. He's just fine. That's my supply closet. It has a window. And I left him some seeds and water."

"Seeds and water," Diane said. "That's cruel."

"How can you be like that?" Donna asked. "Locking someone up and giving him seeds to eat!"

"And I'll bet he broke his leg trying to climb out the window," Gary said.

8

Max laughed. He reached for his keys and opened the closet door. "I'd like to introduce you to Jackie," he said.

The twins looked inside the closet. They saw a large gray bird with a short red tail. He was standing on a perch inside a large cage. The floor of the cage was covered with empty sunflower seed shells and small pieces of apple.

Max told the twins, "Little Jackie is Dr. Jack Cassel's bird. Dr. Cassel is away on vacation and asked me to take care of Jackie."

The legs of the cage had wheels. Max pulled the cage into the lobby. Then he told the twins, "Jackie is an African Gray parrot. Of all the parrots, the African Grays are the best talkers. Jackie learned to talk in Dr. Cassel's office." Then Max whispered, "He thinks he's a doctor, too. Watch."

Max leaned forward and said to Jackie, "I don't feel well."

"Tell me where it hurts," Jackie said. "Tell me where it hurts."

"It's my stomach," Max said.

"You eat too much! You eat too much! You eat too much!"

The twins laughed.

Max pulled the cage close to one of the lobby benches. He sat down and said, "Now tell me about the talent show."

Donna said, "We have some really great acts. Brian Baker will sing 'The Torn Shoes Blues.' He has a great voice. Susie Hannah will dance. Jason Hoffman will read poetry."

"And I have some great magic tricks," Gary said. "Wait here. I'll show them to you."

Gary walked into the elevator. He pressed the button for the fourth floor. As the elevator doors closed, Diane whispered to Max, "Gary plans to be a magician when he's an adult. But I think he'll change his mind soon. Last week he wanted to be an animal doctor. And before that he wanted to be a comedian."

The front door opened. Mr. and Mrs. Wilson walked across the lobby toward the elevator.

"Look at the pretty bird," Mrs. Wilson said.

"Take two aspirin. Take two aspirin," Little Jackie told the Wilsons.

"I think I will," Mr. Wilson said as he waited for the elevator.

The Wilsons took the elevator to the second floor. When it came down again and the doors opened, Gary walked out. He was wearing a black top hat and cape. He was carrying a chalkboard and a large bed sheet. He put it all on one of the lobby chairs.

"You're the MC," he whispered to Donna. "Introduce me."

Donna tapped lightly a few times on one of her school books. Then she said in a loud voice, "And now, straight from the fourth floor, Gary Young, the great magician."

Gary bowed and his hat fell off. He picked it up and showed it to Max, Donna, Diane, and Kevin. The hat seemed to be empty. But then Gary reached into it and pulled out a big red scarf.

Gary put the hat on his head. He picked up the chalkboard and a piece of white chalk.

"And now," he said, "before your very eyes, this white chalk will write red."

Max looked at the piece of chalk. He turned it over. Then he shook his head and said, "It can't be done."

Gary smiled. He took the chalk from Max and wrote the word "red" on the board.

"And now for my greatest trick."

Gary stood near the closet. He held the sheet over his head. The sheet dropped to the floor and Gary was gone.

Max, Donna, Diane, and Kevin applauded. "Come out and take a bow," Donna said.

Gary came out of the closet. He put one hand in front of his waist and the other behind his back. He bowed.

"Take a deep breath," Jackie said. "How do you feel?"

Gary turned to the bird and said, "I feel good, but I think my magic act is missing something."

"Stick out your tongue," the bird told Gary.

Gary stuck out his tongue. Then he pulled it in and said, "If I want to be a magician, I need some better tricks."

Diane said, "Real magicians have cute animals in their acts. They pull rabbits from hats."

Gary looked at Little Jackie. Little Jackie looked at Gary. "I know what I'll do," Gary said. "I'll use Jackie. I'll make *him* disappear!"

CHAPTER THREE

"You can't use Jackie," Max said. He folded his arms. "Dr. Cassel made me promise to take good care of him."

"But nothing will happen to Jackie. I disappeared and nothing happened to me."

"How did he do that?" Diane asked Donna. Donna shook her head. She didn't know.

"I'll cut two flaps in a large cardboard box," Gary told Max. "I'll lift one flap and put Jackie in the box. Then, while I talk to the audience, someone will take Jackie out of the other flap."

"Well," Max said as he unfolded his arms, "that doesn't sound dangerous. You'll have to let me see the box. And I'll have to be at the show to make sure nothing happens to Jackie."

For the next two weeks Diane and Kevin practiced juggling.

Donna borrowed joke books from the library and read them. She wrote the best jokes on small white cards. And as Donna walked home from school, she kept saying, "We are proud to present." Then she pointed to someone nearby. Most people walked quickly ahead. But one woman bowed and did a little dance.

Gary worked on his disappearing box.

Someone in the apartment building had bought a new television set. Gary found the box outside near the trash cans. He taped the box closed. Then he cut two large flaps. Gary painted the box red. And he painted black bars on the box, to make it look like a cage.

Gary and Kevin practiced the disappearing trick in their kitchen. Gary draped a large cloth over a table. Kevin hid under the cloth. Then Gary put his "disappearing box" on the table.

Gary held a teddy bear in his arms. He opened the front flap. "Say good-bye to everyone," Gary said to the bear. Then he put the bear inside the box and let the flap drop down. As soon as the front flap was closed, Kevin opened the back flap and took the bear out.

Later Gary showed the box to Max. Max watched as Gary and Kevin practiced the trick with Jackie.

On the Monday evening of the talent show, people came to the school theater early. Half an hour before the show was to begin, people were already sitting in their seats and waiting. The curtains on the stage were closed. Behind the curtains fifth graders were getting ready.

A boy was singing, "My shoes are worn." In front of him Diane and Kevin were juggling plastic bowling pins. A girl danced in circles with a broom. Children were reading poetry, telling jokes, and one boy was playing a harmonica. And Jackie was in his cage talking to them all.

Ms. Benson, one of the fifth grade teachers, stood on a box. She clapped her hands together and said, "It's time for the show to begin. You'll have to clear the stage. And you'll have to be quiet."

Ms. Benson got off the box. Donna walked in front of the curtains to the center of the

stage. She waited. A few people in the audience saw Donna and told the others to be quiet.

"Welcome to the fifth grade talent show," Donna said. "Before our first act I want to tell you what my parents gave me for my birthday. It was an electric toothbrush. Next year they're giving me electric teeth."

Donna waited. No one laughed.

"And now," she said, "we present a great singer, Brian Baker."

The curtains opened. Brian walked forward, holding a microphone. He sang, "My shoes are worn. My shoes are torn."

Jackie was in his cage in the offstage area, where the audience couldn't see him. Max and Gary stood next to the cage and waited. Kevin and Diane waited in another area off the stage.

The audience cheered when Brian finished singing his "Torn Shoes Blues." Brian bowed a few times. Then Donna introduced the next act.

Kevin looked through the curtain along the side of the stage. "Susie Hannah is dancing with a broom," Kevin whispered to Diane. "We won't be on for a while. Let's go somewhere and practice."

Kevin and Diane walked into the hall. They practiced their juggling act. Then they sat on the floor and rested.

"Donna shouldn't tell those jokes," Diane said. "No one thinks they're funny."

Diane and Kevin talked for a while. Then Kevin jumped up. "I have to get onto the stage," he said.

"Why? We're not on yet."

"Not to juggle. When Gary is on, I have to take Jackie out of the disappearing box. I stand behind the curtain," Kevin told Diane. "Then as soon as Gary puts Jackie into the box, I take him out. I wait for him to show everyone that the box is empty. Then I put Jackie back in the box and Gary shows everyone that Jackie is back."

Diane followed Kevin. They looked at the stage from one of the side doors. Gary was doing his act in front of the closed curtain.

"He's doing the disappearing act," Kevin said. "I've got to get Jackie out of that box."

Kevin ran to the back part of the stage.
He reached through the break in the curtain
and opened the flap in the disappearing box.
He reached for Jackie. But Jackie was gone.

CHAPTER FOUR

" And now," Gary said, "I will bring the bird back."

"No. Don't do it. Jackie's not here," Kevin whispered from the other side of the curtain.

Gary opened the front flap of the box. He reached in. But Jackie wasn't there. He let the front flap drop down again.

Gary waited. Then he turned to the break in the curtain and said real loud, "And now I will bring the bird back."

Gary opened the front flap again. Kevin opened the back flap. He stuck his head into the box and said, "I don't have Jackie. I don't know where he is."

A few people sitting in the front rows saw Kevin. They laughed.

Gary stuck his head into the box and said, "But you took Jackie out of the box."

"No, I didn't."

Everyone was laughing as Donna came onto the stage. "I have to introduce the next act," she told Gary.

Gary walked quickly through the break in the curtain. Max was already there.

"I don't know what happened," Gary told him. "I did everything just the way we practiced."

"And when I got here to take Jackie out, he was already gone," Kevin said.

"Excuse us. Out of our way," two boys said. They were carrying Gary's disappearing box and the table off the stage. "We

have to get this place ready for the next act."

"You'll have to get off the stage," a girl said. She was wearing a short skirt and ballet slippers. She stood on her toes, held her hands over her head, and waited.

Gary, Kevin, Diane, and Max walked quickly off the stage. The curtain opened. Ms. Benson played a tune on the piano, and the girl danced on her toes.

Diane whispered, "I'll bet someone stole Jackie. He's a valuable bird."

"We have to check the exits," Max said.

Max and Gary ran to the back exit, then to the side exits. Diane and Kevin ran to the front exit. A teacher was sitting there behind a desk.

"Did someone carrying a gray talking bird leave here?" Diane asked.

"What?"

"Did anyone leave here carrying something big enough to hold a parrot?" Kevin asked.

"No. No one has come through here since the show began."

Kevin and Diane met Max and Gary in the hall behind the stage.

"Whoever took Jackie didn't go out the front exit," Kevin said.

"And he didn't go out through the back or side exits either," Gary said.

"Well, then, Jackie and whoever took him must be somewhere in the building," Max said.

Kevin and Diane walked off to search the first floor. Max and Gary went upstairs to search the second and third floors.

The doors to the classrooms on the second and third floors were all locked. Max and Gary searched the halls, stairways, and bathrooms. They didn't find anyone.

Max and Gary went downstairs. As they walked toward the theater, they saw Kevin

and Diane crouched near the open door of a classroom.

Diane saw Max and Gary. She held up her hand and signaled them to stop walking. Then slowly and quietly Diane walked to them.

Diane whispered, "We saw someone wearing a bright yellow sweater walk into that classroom. And he was pushing a really big box."

"Well," Max said as he walked toward the open door, "if he has Jackie in that box, he's in real trouble."

CHAPTER FIVE

Max walked quickly into the classroom. Gary, Kevin, and Diane followed him. There was an older man in the room. He was bent over, picking up something.

"Where's Jackie?" Max asked.

The man in the yellow sweater stood up. He was holding a piece of paper. "All the children are in the theater," he said, and dropped the paper into the box.

Diane looked in the box and said, "It's full of trash."

"Sure it's full of trash," the man said. "I'm cleaning the school. That's my job."

"We're looking for a large gray bird," Kevin told the man.

"I just fed all the birds, and the fish, too. And I put the food back in my closet."

Gary told the man, "This bird was part of a magic act in the talent show, and he's missing."

"Oh. There are some birds and fish in the kindergarten rooms. But I don't think they're part of any magic act."

"We're looking for a large gray bird that talks," Max said. "If you see him, please let us know."

The man began to sweep as Max, Gary, Kevin, and Diane left the room. "A talking bird," the old man said as he swept. "I wonder what it says."

There was a chair in the hall outside the principal's office. Max sat on it, rubbed his forehead, and said, "No one has seen Jackie leave, so he must be in the building. But where?"

"Maybe he's flying around the building," Gary said.

Kevin said, "Or maybe someone found him or took him out of the disappearing box and hid him. Then, when everyone leaves, he'll leave, too. But he'll have Jackie."

"The sixth graders have lockers," Diane

said. "Maybe someone put Jackie in one. They have air vents. After the show he'll open the locker and take Jackie home."

Max rubbed his forehead again. Then he told Kevin and Diane, "You check the theater. See if someone there is hiding Jackie. Gary and I will check the lockers and the rest of the building."

Max looked into the stairwell.

Gary walked down the hall to a row of lockers built into the wall. The lockers were tall enough for a coat to hang inside. Gary tapped on one locker and asked, "Are you in there, Jackie?" Gary put his ear against the locker and listened. Then he tapped on the next locker and talked to it.

Kevin and Diane walked into the theater. People were cheering. A boy bowed and the curtains closed. Then Donna walked onto the stage. She held up her hands and asked, "Do you know why ducks don't fly upside down? If they did, they'd quack up."

No one in the audience laughed.

"That's a terrible joke," Diane whispered to Kevin.

"Sh," Kevin whispered back. "Just look for someone with a large bag or box."

Kevin went quietly to the aisle on one side of the theater. Diane went to the aisle on the other side.

A boy walked onto the stage. He smiled and said, "My first poem is called 'How I Make My Lunch.' "

The boy took a paper from his pocket and read:

> " 'Put the peanuts in my shoe.'
> *That's what I told my mother.*
> *Then when I walk to school,*
> *I'll make some peanut butter.*"

Kevin saw a woman sitting in the middle of the back row. There was a large bag on her lap.

"What's in there?" Kevin asked her.

The woman began pulling things out of the bag. "Spinach," she said as she held it up. "Potato chips, carrots, tomatoes, jelly."

"Sh," the people sitting near her said.

"Thank you," Kevin whispered.

"My next poem is called 'I Have a Cold,'" the boy standing on the stage said. He turned over the paper he was holding and read:

*"When I'm in class
and about to sneeze,
I run outside
and water the trees."*

Diane walked quietly from row to row. She saw her parents sitting with her brothers, Eric and Howie. Eric's friend Cam Jansen was there, too. Some people sitting in the theater were holding raincoats. But Diane didn't see any large boxes or bags. Then she heard someone say, "Take two aspirin."

Diane waved to Kevin. They both ran to the back of the theater.

"I think I heard Jackie," Diane told Kevin. "Come with me and I'll show you where he is."

CHAPTER SIX

Diane and Kevin walked quickly down the aisle. Then Diane stopped and whispered, "This is where I heard someone say, 'Take two aspirin.'"

Kevin looked at the man sitting closest to him. Near his feet was a small briefcase. Kevin bent down, as if he were tying his shoelace. He put his ear next to the brief-case and listened.

The man looked down at Kevin and asked, "What are you doing?"

"We're looking for a parrot," Diane told him.

"Oh," the man said and smiled. Then he bent close to Kevin and Diane and whispered, "I have a kangaroo in there, two lions, a polar bear, four rabbits, and a zebra. I wanted a parrot, too, but there wasn't room."

Kevin and Diane smiled. Then they looked at the other people sitting in the row. A small boy and a woman were sitting next to the man.

"They're looking for a parrot," the man said.

"Parrots live in jungles," the boy told Kevin and Diane.

"Here's the aspirin," a man sitting on the other side of the aisle said.

"That's Jackie," Diane said. But when she turned and saw the man, Diane realized she had made a mistake. The man gave the woman sitting next to him two aspirin tablets. She held them carefully as she left the theater.

"Look over there," Kevin whispered to Diane. He pointed two rows ahead to a woman in a green jacket. On the seat beside her was a very large shopping bag. As they walked toward the woman, she stood up. She took the shopping bag and walked to the other aisle.

Kevin and Diane were about to chase after the woman when they heard Donna announce, "And now, for our final act, the fifth grade is proud to present the juggling team of Diane Shelton and Kevin Young."

People clapped as the curtains opened. Kevin and Diane ran onto the stage. Each one waited for the other to throw a bowling pin so they could begin juggling.

"I'll get them," Diane said, and she ran off the stage.

Kevin stood on the stage. He looked at all the people sitting in the theater, waiting

for him to do something. Kevin smiled. But no one smiled back. They just stared.

Kevin reached into his pocket and pretended to pull something out. He pretended to pull something out of two other pockets. Then he juggled the invisible things he took from his pockets.

"You can't really juggle," a boy in the front row called out.

Just then Diane threw a bowling pin to Kevin. He caught it. Kevin threw it back and caught the next one. The bowling pins flew faster and faster between Kevin and Diane. Ms. Benson played a tune on the piano. She played faster and faster.

Diane caught the last bowling pin. The music stopped and the audience cheered.

Donna walked onto the stage. She led Kevin and Diane to the front part of the stage as the curtains closed behind them.

"Weren't they great?" Donna asked the audience.

"Weren't they *all* great?" she asked as the curtains opened again. Standing behind Donna were all the children who had been in the show.

People in the audience cheered. Some got up and began to leave the theater.

Kevin and Diane ran off the stage. Gary and Max ran after them.

"Quick," Kevin said. "Run to the exits."

Diane said, "Look for a woman in a green

jacket. She has a shopping bag big enough to hold Jackie."

Kevin and Diane tried to get through the crowd quickly. It wasn't easy. The people ahead of them wouldn't let them pass.

"Young man," a woman holding a baby told Kevin, "you'll just have to wait." Then she looked at Kevin and Diane. "You're the children who did that clever juggling act. Aren't you?"

"Yes," Diane said. She began to walk past the woman.

Kevin rushed ahead.

Adults and children were standing and talking in the front hall of the school. Kevin and Diane looked for someone carrying a large box or bag. Then their teacher, Ms. Benson, saw them. She was talking with Mr. and Mrs. Shelton. Ms. Benson waved to Diane.

"You go talk to her," Kevin said to Diane. "I'll watch the front exit."

44

"Did you know," Ms. Benson asked Diane, "that the year I taught your brother Eric and his friend Jennifer Jansen was my first year as a teacher?"

Diane smiled.

Ms. Benson held Diane's hand and told her parents, "Your daughter is an excellent student."

Kevin reached the front exit. The teacher there told him that very few people had left. And she hadn't seen anyone carrying a large box or bag.

Kevin waited by the exit. A few minutes later Diane was standing next to him. They watched as people left the school.

Gary ran with Max to the back exit. Many of the fifth graders were there. They were talking about the show and waiting for their parents.

"Look," Gary whispered to Max. "There's someone with a shopping bag."

Max looked through the crowd of children. He saw a woman in a green jacket carrying a large shopping bag.

"That's the woman Diane told us about," Max said. "We have to stop her before she leaves the building."

CHAPTER SEVEN

" Excuse me. Excuse me," Max and Gary said as they walked past children toward the woman in the green jacket.

"Do you have Jackie in there?" Gary asked the woman.

"What's that? Jackie? No, I don't think I have Jackie in here," the woman said as she bent down and reached into the bag.

She pulled out an old pair of sneakers and said, "I wore these when I was in high school. Now I'm giving them to 'I Like to

Help.' It's a group that helps poor people. Look what else I'm giving them."

The woman gave the sneakers to Gary. "Hold these," she told him. Then she took three bright red shirts out of the bag and said, "My children wore these whenever we traveled. I could always find them with these on."

The woman gave the shirts to Gary to hold.

"We really have to go now," Max told the woman.

"But look at this teddy bear. It was my son's favorite. There's a bell inside the bear's tummy."

Gary gave the sneakers and shirts to the woman. Then he and Max walked quickly to the back exit. They watched the fifth graders and their parents leave the building. No one was carrying a bag or box big enough to hold Jackie. After everyone had gone, they walked slowly back to the theater.

Kevin and Diane were sitting in the front row of the theater. When they saw Gary and Max, Kevin shook his head. They hadn't found Jackie.

Gary said, "Maybe someone took Jackie and is hiding until everyone has gone."

"Where would he hide?" Diane asked. "All the classrooms are locked, and we checked the halls and the bathrooms."

"I don't think he's stolen," Kevin said. "I think Jackie is lost. But where could he be?"

Diane, Kevin, Gary, and Max watched as the old man in the yellow sweater pulled a large box down the aisle. He picked up papers and threw them into the box. And he swept.

Donna walked onto the stage. Ms. Benson and the principal, Dr. Smiley, were with her. They talked for a while. Then Donna left the stage and walked toward the others.

"They said it was a great show," Donna

49

told them. "And Dr. Smiley thought my jokes were real funny."

"Jackie is missing," Diane told her sister. "What?"

"He *really* disappeared," Gary said. "We haven't seen him since I put him in my disappearing box."

Donna sat in one of the theater seats. "I think I heard him," she said. "When Gary was onstage, a lot of the kids in the show were laughing. I thought they were laughing at one of my jokes. But I remember hearing, 'Tell me where it hurts,' and, 'Oh, Doctor, save me.' "

Gary stood up and said, "That's Jackie. Why didn't you catch him?"

"I was offstage on this side," Donna said and pointed to the left. "And the laughing was on that side." Donna pointed to the right. "And I was busy. An MC is real important. She has to watch every act and go onstage at just the right time."

50

"Let's look for him," Gary said.

"Where?" Kevin asked. "We've looked just about everyplace."

The old man in the yellow sweater pulled the box to the front of the theater. He picked up a few papers and showed them to Max.

The old man said, "I wish they wouldn't give out programs for these shows. They all end up on the floor."

Max, Gary, Kevin, and Donna helped the old man pick up the programs. Diane began to help. But she stopped. She looked at the old man and rubbed her chin. Then she asked him, "Did you say before that you have a closet like Max has, where you keep all your brooms and things?"

"Sure."

"And you keep bird food there, too?"

"Yes, and I have fish food and plant food in the closet, too. Sometimes plants need extra minerals to help them grow."

"Would you please take us there?"

CHAPTER EIGHT

The old man pulled a large ring of keys from his pocket. "The closet is locked," he said as he walked through the door near the front of the theater. "I try to keep it locked when there are children in the building."

"But while you're cleaning, you have to open it sometimes, don't you?" Diane asked. "And you might even forget and leave it open for a while."

Diane was walking beside the old man.

Kevin, Gary, Donna, and Max were right behind them.

"Sure, I open it. All my mops and brooms and things are in there."

"And the food for the fish and birds," Diane said.

"We did keep it in the kindergarten rooms. But the children kept feeding the animals. They made a mess, and the animals were getting sick from eating too much. Now I keep the food in my closet."

The old man stopped in front of a metal door with the number 157 painted on it. As he turned the key in the lock, someone on the other side of the door said, "Stick out your tongue. Take a deep breath. Say 'Ah.' Tell me where it hurts."

"Jackie!" Gary, Kevin, Donna, Diane, and Max all called out.

"It sounds like there's a doctor locked in here," the old man said as he opened the door. He turned on the light.

"Oh, Doctor, save me," Jackie called.

"Just look at this mess," the old man said. The floor was covered with papers. Open boxes of fish food and bird food were spilled on the floor. "How did that bird get in here? He's worse than the children."

"Jackie probably flew out of the disappearing box by himself and you probably left this door open for a while," Diane said. "Jackie saw the food and flew right in."

Max was standing just outside the closet. He held out his hand and said, "Come to me, Jackie."

Jackie flew toward Max. But he kept on flying.

"Quick! Catch him," Gary called as he ran after Jackie.

Jackie flew toward the theater. Gary and the others ran after him.

"I'll get the cage," Max said, and he ran into the theater.

Jackie flew into an open stairwell. When the twins got there, Jackie was gone.

"He could be anywhere," Kevin said. "These stairs go to every floor in the building."

The twins ran up the stairs. Gary and Kevin ran through the second floor halls. Diane and Donna ran through the third floor. Max ran out of the theater carrying the cage.

Each of the twins ran from one floor to the next. They ran past each other. But they didn't find Jackie. They all met in the third floor stairwell and walked downstairs together.

"Maybe Max found him," Kevin said.

As the twins walked to the theater, they passed the principal's office. "It's these children," they heard Dr. Smiley say. "Some of them do the strangest things. They give me a headache."

"Take two aspirin," they heard Jackie tell the principal. Then they heard the principal and Max laugh.

The twins walked into the principal's office. Max was sitting in a chair. Jackie was in his cage.

"I found Jackie in here talking to Dr. Smiley," Max told the twins.

"This bird is great," Dr. Smiley said. "Listen to this."

Dr. Smiley sat on the edge of his desk near Jackie's cage. "What should I tell my teachers?" he asked Jackie.

"Take a deep breath. Stick out your tongue."

The fourth floor twins stood around Jackie's cage.

"Why did you fly away, Little Jackie?" Donna asked.

"You had us all worried," Diane told Jackie.

"Oh, Doctor, save me. Save me," Jackie called out.

"I didn't save you," Dr. Smiley said.

Then the twins and Max all said together, "We did!"